Introduction

Ned the Narwhal Voyages the 5 Oceans is a story about a naughty narwhal named Ned, who has a rainbow horn and special flipper wings!

He flies and swims around the world, meeting new animal characters and learning valuable life lessons in this exciting ocean adventure!

ISBN: 978-1-7362829-6-0

Library of Congress Control Number: 2021903301

The Llove Llama & Friends Series

The Llove Llama Travels the 7 Continents

Ned the Narwhal Voyages the 5 Oceans

Bob the Sloth Explores South America

Ruby the Red Panda Discovers Asia

Donut the Dingo Dog Walks About Australia

Charli the Cheetah Races Through Africa

Peppermint the Penguin Protects Antarctica

Brave Feather the Owl Scouts Europe

www.TheLloveLlamaAndFriends.com

Dedications

For Nana, **Joan Black**, an ever-glowing light in my life,

Paw Paw, **Willis Black** aka "Blackie",

who taught me that family is more than a word,

and for my shining stars – **Piper, Finnian, Greer, and Noirin**

~ SC ~

For my parents, **Ron and Roseanne Talbot**,

who gave so much and asked for so little.

Thank you, Dad, for your strength and love "through the years".

Thank you, Mom, for always being my angel.

~ MTK ~

Ned the Narwhal
Voyages the 5 Oceans

Written by

Monica Talbot-Kerkes & Sharla Charpentier

Illustrated by

Aljon Inertia

Original Character Sketches by Sharla Charpentier

Arctic
Ocean

The ARCTIC OCEAN is very cold,
at the top of the world, near the North Pole.
Narwhals swim and play all day,
listening and dancing to Rock 'n' Roll.

One special day the narwhals were amazed,
when Ned the Narwhal was born.
Ned had wings for flippers!
And a rainbow unicorn horn!

No narwhal had wings like Ned.
He had the longest horn to be seen!
His horn was pink, yellow, and orange,
red, purple, blue, and green.

Ned had a shiny mirror.
It was a gigantic block of ice!
Ned always gazed at himself
and thought, "WOW, do I look nice."

Ned had only one friend.
She was Peeps the Polar Bear!
Peeps had sparkly tap shoes
and wore a tiara in her hair.

"The Arctic is SOOOOO boring," Ned complained.
Peeps twirled and tap danced on the ice.
She peeped, "Explore all the other oceans!
I bet they're super fun and nice!!!"

Ned remembered The Llove Llama,
and how she traveled the world.
If The Llove Llama could do it,
NED THE NARWHAL could give it a whirl!

Ned flew to the PACIFIC OCEAN.
It was the biggest ocean ever!
Ned dove down to the sandy bottom.
HOLY JELLYFISH! A hidden treasure!

It was a buried treasure box
by a pirate ship sunk in the sea.
WOW! Gold coins and silver shells!
Ned said, "HAH! No one is as rich as ME!"

It was King Simon the Shark!
He wore a diamond crown of teeth.
King Simon grinned at Ned and said,
"Mmmmm. You look like a nice bite of meat."

King Simon the Shark swam closer.
Ned zipped up to the top!
PHEW! His flipper wings had saved him!
Into the bright blue sky he popped!

"It's not a stinger!!!" Ned said madly.
"Can't you see it's a gorgeous horn?!"
Cliff brushed his mustache with a shell
and fed Eddie an ear of sea corn.

Ned soared to the SOUTHERN OCEAN.
There were icebergs everywhere.
Ned landed on a huge one and yelled,
"Hellooooo? Is anyone out there???"

A voice said, "How ya doin' Pal?"
It was Lucky the Leopard Seal!
Lucky threw Ned a beach ball,
jumped up and did a cartwheel.

Southern
Ocean

"Let's have some fun!" Lucky cheered.
He pushed Ned down the icy hill.
They sled and played all night long!
Ned said, "PLEASE! I need to chill!"

Lucky exclaimed, "What?! Are you nuts?!
We party and play all year!!!"
Ned said, "Sorry, it's not my thing.
Are there any narwhals here?"

"Nope, no narwhals," Lucky said.
"Mostly penguins, puffins, and whales."
Ned felt tired and out of place.
He sighed, "Time for me to sail."

Ned sailed to the INDIAN OCEAN.
It was light blue and quite hot.
Ned landed on an island and said,
"This looks like a better spot."

Ned took a nice long nap.
BONK! Something hit his head!
It was Sophie the Sea Turtle!
"Oh, why excuse me," Sophie said.

Sophie's shell was many colors.
She swam gently and very slow.
Under the shimmery water,
she looked like an ocean rainbow.

"We are so beautiful!" Ned said.
Sophie looked him in the eye.
"Why does that matter?" she asked.
Then naughty Ned started to cry.

"Don't you think I'm special?" Ned sobbed.
"Don't you think I'm cool?"
"Don't you think I'm amazing?"
Sophie said, "No, you're just a fool."

"Color doesn't matter.
You see, everyone is equal.
We are ALL special and unique –
ANIMALS, BIRDS, FISH, and PEOPLE."

She gave Ned a sea tissue.
"Now wipe away your tears.
It's never too late to change.
You have many, many years."

Sophie smiled and swam away.
Ned finally began to see.
"Sophie is right," Ned thought.
"EVERYONE IS SPECIAL! Not just me!"

Ned sped back to the Arctic.
He cried, "PLEASE FORGIVE ME!"
The other narwhals did, of course.
Now Ned is happy as can be!!!

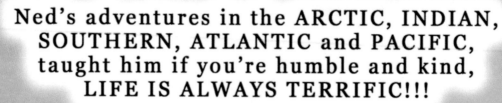

Ned's adventures in the ARCTIC, INDIAN,
SOUTHERN, ATLANTIC and PACIFIC,
taught him if you're humble and kind,
LIFE IS ALWAYS TERRIFIC!!!

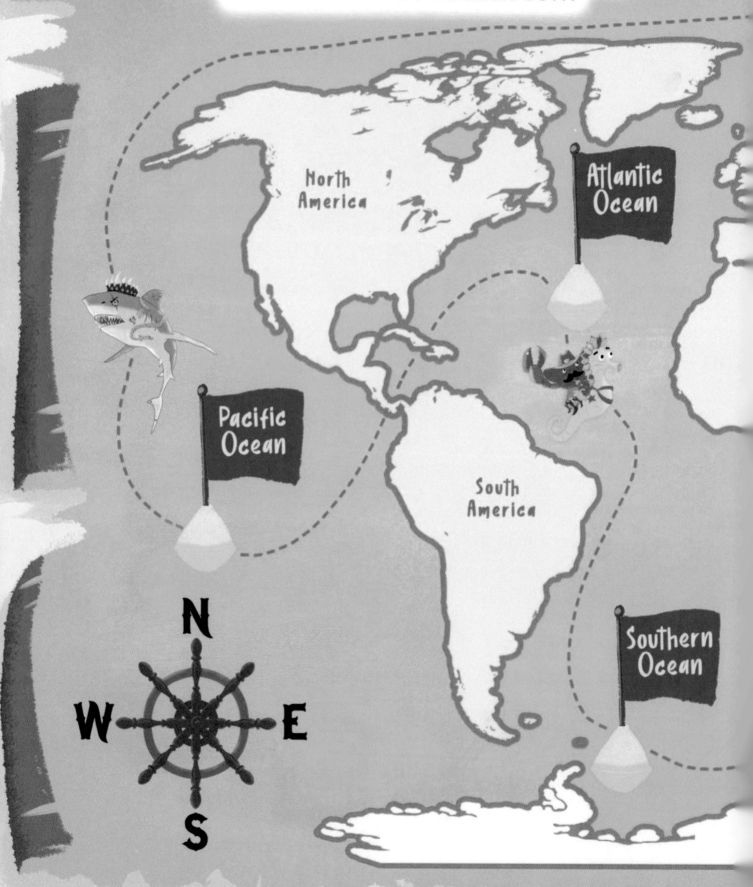

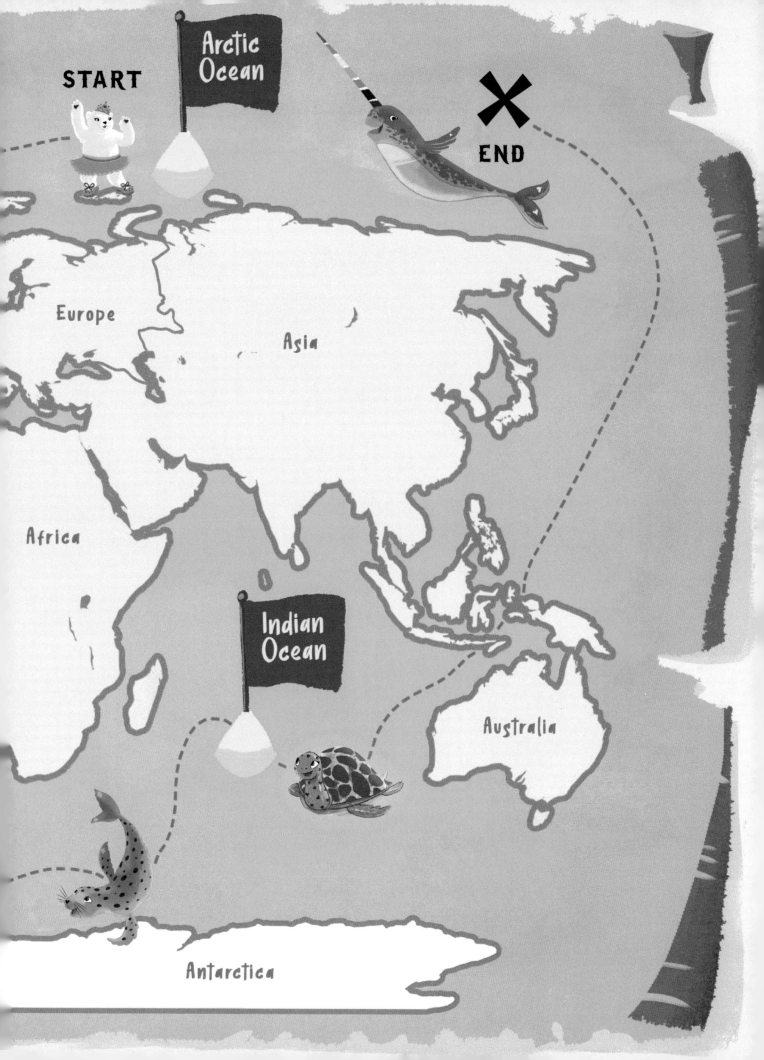

START

Arctic Ocean

END

Europe

Asia

Africa

Indian Ocean

Australia

Antarctica

Now Ned the Narwhal is home.
But this story isn't the end!
It's time to head to SOUTH AMERICA
TO HANG OUT WITH BOB & HIS NEW FRIENDS!

Discussion Questions

1. What are the 5 oceans? Which 2 oceans border the USA?

2. Which of the 5 oceans do narwhals live in? Describe the habitat where narwhals live.

3. Why does Ned want to leave his ocean home? What difficulties does he encounter on his voyage? What do you do when you are upset?

4. Which ocean does Ned meet Sophie the Sea Turtle in? What does she teach Ned? What does it mean to be humble?

5. Can you think of any threats to oceans? How can humans help save marine life?

6. Explain at least one lesson Ned learns on his trip around the world. How does Ned change after his voyage?

7. The other narwhals forgive Ned when he returns home. Why is forgiveness important?

8. Which oceans would you like to voyage to? Why?

Narwhals

Habitat: Narwhals are found in the Arctic Ocean.

Facts

❖ The narwhal is a species of whale. People often refer to a narwhal as the "unicorn of the sea" because of its long horn.

❖ The horn, most commonly found on males, is actually a tooth that can grow up to 9 feet! Some even have 2!

❖ A group of narwhals is called a 'blessing'.

Threats: Narwhals are not endangered as of yet. However, they have been identified as 'special concern', meaning they could easily become endangered.

Polar Bears

Habitat: Polar bears are only found in the Arctic.

Facts

❖ Polar bears are the largest land carnivores. They can grow up to 10 feet tall and weigh up to a ton (2000 lbs.) – about the size of a small car!

❖ Polar bears are excellent swimmers and can swim for days at a time!

❖ Polar bears' skin is actually black. The fur has no color at all. It looks white because it reflects light.

Threats: Scientists now believe polar bears are vulnerable to extinction mostly due to climate change. Polar bears are losing their habitat because ice is thinning and melting faster.

Crabs

Habitat: Crabs live in all 5 oceans of the world.

Facts

❖ Crabs are known as the "spiders of the sea" because like spiders, crabs have legs that bend at joints.

❖ Crabs walk sideways so they don't trip over their own legs!

❖ Female crabs can lay up to 100,000 eggs!

Threats: There are currently dozens of crab species listed as critically endangered. Beach development and overharvesting for use as bait are examples of how humans threaten the survival of crabs.

Seahorses

Habitat: Seahorses are found in tropical and mild coastal ocean waters.

Facts

❖ Seahorses are known as the "jewels of the ocean" and are tiny fish.

❖ Male seahorses actually carry the eggs. Baby seahorses are about the size of an M&M!

❖ Seahorses are experts in camouflage. Some change color to hide in their coral reef habitat.

Threats: Two species of seahorses are endangered and more are identified as "vulnerable". Examples of threats to seahorses are habitat loss, water pollution, climate change, overfishing, and illegal souvenir trading.

Sharks

Habitat: Sharks live in all 5 oceans of the world.

Facts

❖ A shark is known as a "swimming nose" because of its great sense of smell.

❖ The female whale shark is the biggest fish in the world, weighing up to 45 tons (90,000 lbs.) — about the size of a school bus!

❖ Sharks have existed unchanged for 400 million years – long before dinosaurs.

Threats: A few shark species are classified as 'vulnerable', while the Scalloped and Great Hammerhead sharks are endangered. Sharks are overfished due to the demand for their fins, meat, and teeth.

Leopard Seals

Habitat: Leopard seals live in the frigid Southern Ocean.

Facts

❖ Leopard seals get their name from their black-spotted coats like leopard cats.

❖ Leopard seals do not have ears! They have 'ear openings' instead.

❖ Orca whales and sharks are the only natural enemies of leopard seals.

Threats: The leopard seal's greatest dangers are habitat loss due to climate change and overfishing of their food chain.

Sea Turtles

Habitat: Sea turtles live in almost every ocean basin throughout the world.

Facts

- ❖ Green sea turtles are known as "ocean lawnmowers" because they eat sea grass and algae.

- ❖ Sea turtles think jellyfish are delicious!

- ❖ Sea turtles cry! They have glands that help to empty salt from their eyes.

Threats: Six of the seven sea turtle species are considered threatened or endangered due to pollution, eating plastic, poaching, overfishing, and entanglement in fishing nets and lines.

Llamas

Habitat: Llamas' natural habitat is the Andes Mountains in South America.

Facts

- ❖ Llamas are related to camels but without the hump!

- ❖ Llamas are brave. They are used as guardians for animals like sheep and alpacas.

- ❖ Scientists have discovered special antibodies that llamas produce which could prevent infections & viruses.

Threats: Thankfully, llamas are not endangered as of yet.

Arctic Ocean

Norway ~ Northern Lights

❖ The Arctic is the smallest, shallowest, and coldest ocean!

❖ The Arctic goes around the North Pole and is mostly covered in ice.

❖ A special feature of the Arctic is the Northern Lights – a vivid color show of the Earth's magnetic field interacting with the sun.

Southern Ocean

Antarctica ~ Southern Ocean

❖ The Southern, also known as the Antarctic Ocean, is the fourth largest ocean.

❖ The Southern is the youngest ocean. It formed when Antarctica separated from South America.

❖ The Southern is the only ocean that wraps around the world!

Atlantic Ocean

Giant's Causeway ~ Northern Ireland

❖ The Atlantic is the second largest ocean. It is about 6.5 times the size of the United States!

❖ The Atlantic is the saltiest of the 5 oceans.

❖ The Atlantic drives our weather patterns, including hurricanes.

Pacific Ocean

Oregon Sand Dunes ~ United States

❖ The Pacific is the largest of the 5 oceans. It is bigger than all 7 continents combined!

❖ Most of the islands in the world are found in the Pacific. That's more than 25,000 islands!

❖ Most of the world's supply of fish is caught in the Pacific.

Indian Ocean

Maldives ~ Indian Ocean

- ❖ The Indian is the third largest ocean. It is about 5.5 times the size of the United States.

- ❖ The Indian Ocean is the warmest of the 5 oceans.

- ❖ About 40% of the world's offshore oil production comes from the Indian Ocean!

DID YOU KNOW THAT THE OCEANS COVER MORE THAN 70% OF THE EARTH?

DID YOU KNOW THAT THE OCEANS ARE HOME TO NEARLY 95% OF ALL LIVING THINGS?

DID YOU KNOW THAT THE OCEANS ARE OUR GREATEST SOURCE OF OXYGEN?

Human activities threaten our oceans & marine life.

YOU CAN HELP!!!

DON'T EVER POLLUTE!

USE LESS PLASTIC! RECYCLE ALL PLASTIC!

VOLUNTEER FOR CLEANUPS AT THE BEACH!

START A FUNDRAISER AT YOUR SCHOOL!

DONATE TO OCEAN PRESERVATION ORGANIZATIONS!

About the Authors

Monica Talbot–Kerkes & Sharla Charpentier

Monica and Sharla are cousins who are making their dreams of writing adventurous and educational children's books come true. Their vision is to inspire, teach, and positively impact children while bringing awareness to world crises and the amazing animals that share our beautiful planet.

Monica is a mother of two, a published author, an English as a Second Language teacher, and poet. She created the original storylines for *The Llove Llama* and *Ned the Narwhal* books and found her imagination and love of rhyme to shine best in children's books.

Sharla is a mother of four, a published author, a lawyer, artist, and poet. She co-authored *The Llove Llama* and *Ned the Narwhal* books and brought to life *The Llove Llama and Friends* characters through her original character sketches.

www.TheLloveLlamaAndFriends.com

 @thellovellama   **thellovellama@gmail.com**   **The_Llove_Llama**

About the Illustrator

Aljon Inertia

Aljon specializes in creating beautiful, one-of-a-kind illustrations for children's books. His goal and purpose in life are to bring his passion for illustration to children's books that speak to good morals and values while providing lessons to today's youth.

Aljon's colorful illustrations bring engagement to the author's content, so the story comes alive on the book's pages. His creative illustrations are published in children's books worldwide.

Follow Aljon on Instagram **@inertiaillustrator**

Made in the USA
Middletown, DE
22 March 2022

63004906R00027